ODE TO CLASSICS

NOCTURNAL SCREAMS VOL 2

Mark Leslie

PUBLISHING

Stark Publishing
Waterloo, Ontario
www.starkpublishing.ca

The characters and events portrayed in this short story
collection are fictitious. Any similarity to real persons, living or
dead, is coincidental and not intended by the author.

ODE TO CLASSICS: Nocturnal Screams Volume 2
Mark Leslie
April 2020

For the masters whose author shoulders all us writers today now stand on.

Table of Contents

Introduction

WHEN I PUBLISHED my first book, *One Hand Screaming*, which is a collection of macabre stories and poems, I confessed to screaming a lot. Silent screams, I called them. I said that story ideas bounced around inside my head like an impending storm, brewing into a force that will escape in a wild dance of chaos if I didn't stop to write them down.

Admittedly, that was a bit dramatic.

But, try as I might, I haven't been able to come up with a better way to describe my conviction to have to write.

And not only to write, but to explore concepts from the darker side of the universe. To pursue the shadows, to call out the fears.

To write, or not to write. There never has been a question.

Whether to suffer the slings and arrows of outrageous ideas that brew within my head or to take pen and paper against the sea of madness, and by capturing them, control them.

To write, to scream no more.

Okay, I got a bit carried away with the *Hamlet* spin-off. And that's something I drew on quite heavily in my full-length novel *I, Death*. (My main character was an angst-filled teenager with Hamlet-like suicidal thoughts as he was trying to come to terms with the death curse he was born with as everyone he gets close to ends up dying)

But reflecting on how that Shakespearean tragedy inspired a good part of a novel I wrote might be perfectly appropriate here, because the stories you are about to read can all be traced back to inspiration that I found from the classics or the master writers who came before me.

"Memento Mori: A Curious Nightmare" was inspired directly (and draws quite heavily upon) the Mark Twain short story "A Curious Dream." I enjoyed the dark humor and underlying moral message that Mark Twain was exploring in the story, but I couldn't help speculating if he pulled too many punches in his delivery. I thus explored a parallel story structure, drawing heavily from the voice, setting and situation, but I added an additional layer of horror far beyond Twain's own curious dream.

One of my favorite short stories of all time is Shirley Jackson's "The Lottery." It is a brilliant execution of conformity gone mad, the concept of focusing on a scapegoat and the fickle manner by which we can so easily be turned upon one another. Inspired to explore a similar world, I wondered how a similar small town might co-exist peacefully with a monster in their midst.

And, wanting to explore how an antiquarian bookish fetish might survive well-past the grave, co-author Kimberly Foottit and I had fun creating professor Marshall Emerson (AKA Professor Prospero), a Shakespearean scholar back from the dead to seek vengeance upon those who dared use digital technology to replicate his precious 1861 folio edition of the Bard's works in our tale "Prospero's Ghost."

But enough introductory talk. You and I have some place to be together: exploring modern horror stories inspired from the masters and the classics.

Memento Mori: A Curious Nightmare
A moral tale dedicated to Mark Twain

THE NIGHT BEFORE last I had a curious nightmare. Apparently, I sat on my doorstep in quiet thought with the hour nearing twelve o'clock. It was a warm evening for the last day of October, and I was relishing in the calm splendor of what might have been the last nice evening to be sitting outside so long with only a thin jacket around my shoulders.

The children, who, earlier that evening, had roamed the streets dressed in the usual garb of witches, ghosts and goblins were by then safely tucked in bed. Gone were their childish cries of excitement. There was not a sound in the air except for a slight wind through the trees and perhaps the distant passing of cars on the highway.

All was just right when, from up the street I could hear a boney clack-clacking. I turned to see what might be making such a strange noise on so quiet a night.

Around the corner appeared a figure, dressed in a moldy, torn shroud, dragging behind him a long box of rotting wood which could only be a coffin. As the figure neared, I could detect the distinct skeletal features of his face from beneath the hooded robe.

Approaching my side, he paused, dropped the burden he had been dragging behind him, and sat on the edge of it. It creaked in protest as he put his weight on it. His jaw, held to his skull with the thinnest layer of sinew, began to clack as he addressed me.

"It is too bad," he said. "Too bad, indeed."

"What is too bad?" I asked. In that manner we all accept strangeness in dreams without a second thought. It never occurred to me that seeing a dead man drag his coffin down the street was an abnormal thing.

He brought a skeletal hand up to scratch his boney chin. "Most things. It is getting to be that I almost wish I had never died."

"Why do you say this? What is wrong?"

"What is wrong? Everything is wrong. Look at this burial shroud; it is now nothing but a rag. And this coffin, once comfortable, is now a rotting box that I can barely hold together. All my possessions are falling apart before your very eyes and you ask what is wrong?"

"Pardon me for saying, but I wouldn't think that, in your state, you would mind such matters."

"Oh," he said, his white boned grin sending shivers down my spine. "You have much to learn about death, my friend – much to learn about what you call my state. The fact is, I do mind such matters. There is an element of pride in death, and comfort is perhaps the only thing left to concern yourself with in the everlasting sleep of death.

"You see, in the early years of the last century, when I laid down to my final sleep, I was happy and at peace. I had myself a strong and sturdy coffin lined in the finest of silks. Above me, I boasted a polished smooth gravestone which had been adorned with fresh flowers and plants by my surviving loved ones. For a while, I was the proudest corpse in all the graveyard. It was a wonderful thing to be dead.

"But see the difference now," he said, and a ghastly expression developed on the decayed features of his face. "My grave is all caved-in, the wood of my coffin has rotted in places so badly that vermin have crawled in through the holes, not to mention the crawly bugs that have taken residence in my silks and what is left of my flesh. My gravestone, marred by time and the elements, now bows forward, as if in disgrace and threatens to fall flat in the moistened, flooded earth. And it has been years since anything other than weeds and vines have graced my stone. My loved ones and descendants, who used to visit me on holidays and anniversaries, have all either died themselves, moved away or forgotten me.

"My headstone itself used to be a thing of pride, reading the simple term: 'GONE TO HIS JUST REWARD.' When first I died, it was a fine epitaph, one to be proud of, for finally, after a hard life, I would sleep in a comfortable, warm and dry place for all of eternity. But now the irony reigns strong. It's also interesting how the grave not two stones away from my own reads 'Death is the starlit strip between the companionship of yesterday and the reunion of tomorrow.' Now despite the awful state of the gravesite, at least the epitaph holds a little bit of hope for my neighbor. But are these decrepit, forgotten graves our just reward now?"

"But," I said. "You are dead."

"Yes," he replied. "Dead and forgotten. And while I lie in a moldy, leaky box with maggots crawling through the sockets where my eyes used to behold the world, how should it be that you lie in a comfortable bed just one block away?"

Unable to answer him, I shook my head.

"Ah yes, I know – because you are alive, and I am dead. You said it yourself a moment ago."

"But it doesn't have to be that way," I insisted. "Perhaps we can do something, the townspeople and me. We can work on the graveyard and restore it to its former glory. There is no need for you to leave. Tomorrow, I'll..."

But he cut me off. "No. No more tomorrows. It is too late, my friend. Much too late. You have all ignored our simple needs for too long now. We've already discussed the situation and the time is now at hand." He paused and grated his teeth in a way that made me shiver. "I have but one thing to say to you. Memento Mori."

Not understanding, I cast a confused look at him, to which he shook his head muttering how little Latin modern folks know and repeated the phrase in words I could understand. "Remember, you will die."

With that said, he pushed past me up the stairs. I turned so that I might stop him but was amazed at how fast he could move his skeletal bones. Before I knew it, he'd entered my home and locked the door behind him. I was locked out of my own house.

The clack-clacking sound arose again, this time in a loud chorus. I turned to spy an entire procession of the dead, each dressed in similar moldy robes and dragging their coffins behind them.

I screamed.

That was when I woke from the nightmare.

As I lay there I thought about the dream, wondering at the moral involved, and then decided that we place too much emphasis on the meaning of dreams. After all, it was probably just the result of a weird combination of food I had ingested and that book of stories by Mark Twain I had read prior to falling asleep. Why couldn't I have dreamed of meeting up with Huck Finn instead?

Shaking the sleep from my eyes, I sat up, and for the first time became aware of a presence in the room with me. The bed in which I typically slept alone was housing another body.

Slowly I turned to find myself face to face with the cavernous sockets of the dead man from my dream. A smile lit upon his face that struck terror in my heart. His skeletal hand lifted from beneath the sheet as he pointed the way out of the bedroom. "Memento Mori," was all that he uttered.

I got out of bed and reached for my bathrobe but found instead a moldy, putrid shroud. Shaking my head, I donned the shroud and sadly moped out of the bedroom as the maggots and bugs sought my warm flesh.

My eyes downcast all the way to the graveyard, I did not bother to look at the others who, like me, were plodding their way down the street. Refuges kicked out of our own homes by the very dead we'd forgotten about, we slugged along like the poor losers we were.

Tired, I walked along through the neglected tombstones, until I found the one that read: GONE TO HIS JUST REWARD. With one last look at the night sky, I sank down into the hole.

And here is where I lie, hoping that this too is another dream from which I will awake. I'm also thinking that the next morning we should all get up and put some work into this graveyard – make it a nice, respectable place to dwell. But I'm tired now, and all that I want for the moment is to sleep.

It's a good idea though. Maybe tomorrow . . .

The Ritual of the Drawing

MR. McNEAL ISN'T an evil person. He just wants to go about a peaceful existence. Everybody in Birks Falls knows that he didn't want to kill those children; he just couldn't fight his own nature.

You see, Mr. McNeal is a vampire.

And, under the proper circumstances, a vampire is a wonderful thing for a town to have. After all, we'd been living in peace with one for generations. And, up until those neighborhood children started disappearing, things had been just fine.

Perhaps I should explain a little bit about how things work here in Birks Falls. To do that, I guess I should start at the beginning, when the people of this town first found out about Mr. McNeal.

It was well over a hundred years ago when they first suspected that the newcomer named McNeal was a vampire. At the time, little was known about vampires. They existed as a part of myths and legends, vague tales told about undead beings stalking the night to drink people's blood. All that the townspeople knew was they wanted to be rid of such a creature. So, afraid and unprepared, armed only with clubs and knives, they banded together and decided to confront McNeal.

When they arrived at McNeal's door, he greeted them. Surprisingly, he knew what they had planned and told them he understood how they could feel that way. We now know that McNeal possessed the power to catch them off guard and quickly destroy them all, as pitifully armed as they were, without garlic or holy water or silver crosses or wooden stakes. But he didn't harm a single soul. Instead, he admitted that he was, indeed, a vampire, and offered to be gone from the town by the following nightfall.

The townspeople were completely shocked. He was nothing like the myths and legends suggested he would be. Instead, he was pleasant and courteous.

Then he shocked them again, by making an offer.

Now I'm not sure of the exact words exchanged; all I know is that by the next day an agreement had been reached. Mr. McNeal would stay in Birks Falls but would not kill any innocent townspeople. Instead, the people of the town would provide him with two adult-sized humans at least once a month. Mr. McNeal couldn't not drink blood — but he could at the very least let them decide whose blood he would consume.

The townspeople saw his offer for what it truly is -- a great way to dispose of society's unwanted -- the criminals, the insane, the unproductive. And the mere thought of what might happen should one cross the line into crime would act as a deterrent. Legend has it that the crime rate dropped dramatically that next year.

It's funny when you think about it, but, having grown up in Birks Falls, it's hard to imagine growing up without a vampire in town. I still remember my mother prodding me to get my schoolwork done. "C'mon Elsie," she would say. "Get cracking at that homework or else I'll send you to see Mr. McNeal." Sometimes, all that a teacher would have to do was make a sucking noise, and all of the children in the classroom would snap to attention.

The fear, of course, grew when everybody became exposed to the now famous vampire novel Dracula. Bram Stoker put into words and horrific images the very fears and whispering the townspeople had engaged in. By then, the threat of "vampire" had an image everyone could appreciate. I'm certain that back in the late 1890's the crime rate must have plummeted even more dramatically.

All that good for so simple a task.

I mean, look at all the benefits we've reaped from this situation by offering up nothing more than twenty-four people per year. Take a look at your own town. Even if your population is as low as 6000, like Birks Falls, I'm sure that you could come up with at least two people every month whom you'd like to send to Mr. McNeal. Perhaps you could come up with two people every week.

The townspeople were able to orchestrate an annual assembly wherein the elders of the town provided the vote as to who was to be selected as the Donated. It then came to be that every New Year's Eve, the entire population of the town over the age of sixteen would gather in front of the town court and participate in *The Ritual of the Drawing*.

All the participant names were written down on slips of paper and placed in a large steel drum. One of the elders would draw twelve names during the final twelve minutes before the stroke of midnight. Those twelve people drawn would be that year's Chosen and would be responsible for delivering the Donated to Mr. McNeal for one month each.

Most people considered it an honor to be among the Chosen. Children grew up longing for the day they turned sixteen so that they too might have a chance at being one of the Chosen. But times are changing, as they often do. Now, there are those who see the honor as some sort of curse of responsibility. They feel they have better things to do than deliver the Donated to their rightful fate. They claim it is a barbaric chore they shouldn't be forced to do. Little do they recognize it is a very civilized custom which maintains order and respect. It is a custom which has made this town a very safe and peaceful place to live and raise a family.

Like most customs, nobody is actually forced to participate. There are no written laws about *The Ritual of the Drawing*. It is merely a tradition which has always been strictly adhered to.

But the fact that it is never enforced, that it relies on mutual trust is probably why this whole mess came about.

You see, just this past year, a fellow named Jed Stevens was drawn as one of the Chosen for the month of May. He is of the younger generation and has the attitude problem I've already mentioned. Yet, despite his attitude, nobody suspected that he simply wouldn't feed Mr. McNeal. Such a thought was . . . well, it was unthinkable at the time. People had protested in the past, but before Jed Stevens came along, nobody had ever not performed their duties as the Chosen.

Jed Stevens had decided he would let both of the Donated go free rather than deliver them to their rightful fate. The results of these "acts of mercy" were the loss of several neighborhood children.

Having not been fed for an entire month, Mr. McNeal grew hungry. Ravenous, in fact. The diet of one adult every two weeks was a considerable cut back for him as it was, so when even that stopped, he was far beyond his limit of self-control. It wasn't his fault that he wasn't being fed. I mean, he had been keeping up with his half of the deal. It was our own fault for not enforcing the Chosen to perform their duties.

So, combine Mr. McNeal's understandable hunger with the presence of the neighborhood children playing on his lawn beyond sunset, and the results are obvious.

Such a tragedy had been avoided for well over a century with our annual *Ritual of the Drawing*. I guess the people of the newest generation, like Jed Stevens, just don't listen, just don't see the necessity of the tradition. They only see that they don't like it and they rebel.

Only, this time, the rebellion cost the town several innocent children. May their souls rest in peace.

Once it was discovered that Jed had shirked his duties and was responsible for the lives of these children, a meeting of the elders was held. It was rapidly decided that I should be the one to take responsibility for Jed Stevens' actions. We had to make sure that an example was made of him so that such a thing would not happen again.

The next day, I lead him, gagged and handcuffed, to the door of Mr. McNeal's home. It was dusk, and the church tower threw a long shadow that grew slowly along Mr. McNeal's front yard as the sun sank. I shuddered, thinking about how the shadow traced a path across the very yard where those children used to play. Such a shame, I thought, wanting to point this out to Jed, but I couldn't look at him. Instead, I continued to stare at the growing shadow until the sun sank completely below the horizon. Then I counted to one hundred for good measure before I knocked.

Mr. McNeal greeted me at the door with a pleasant smile. I had never seen him up close before and was amazed with how attractive he was. He was a handsome man, even though his hair was thin and speckled with grey. His face looked like it was carved from a soft wood, delicate and smooth to touch, yet his eyes were sharp and bright. His smile revealed a perfect set of pearly white teeth. Human-looking teeth, not the sharp, blood-stained incisors out of vampire movies.

He wore a pale grey dinner jacket with a red ascot about his neck and navy-blue Ivy League styled pants. On his feet he wore what looked like penny loafers. I was perplexed. Despite his sophisticated manner, his dress was of a combination I'd never seen thrown together before. But despite the collage of style, it was pleasing to look at just the same.

His eyes never left mine as his smile straightened then threatened to become a frown. He knew why we were here. For a moment, I thought he was going to turn us away and say that it was too late. No more *Ritual of the Drawing*. No more mercy. No more peaceful co-existence.

Then, he smiled again, and I realized I had been holding my breath. I breathed again, appreciating his smile. He was very becoming and looked to be in his mid-fifties, less than ten years older than myself. I'm certain, also, that I caught a look in his face that moment which reminded me of my late husband. I felt a pang of loss and shame at that thought, but quickly pushed it aside.

Silently, Mr. McNeal gestured for us to follow him, and turned to lead us into the living room. It was decorated in a similarly cross-cultural/cross-time fashion. But I had no time to really admire the premises, for my eyes remained mostly on Mr. McNeal. He was fascinating. It was as if I could not look at him enough.

I sat down on a rocking chair while Mr. McNeal took Jed by the arm and sat with him on the sofa. He offered me a cup of tea, which I accepted.

When Mr. McNeal left, I tried to keep my eyes from Jed's. He attempted to speak but the gag prevented it. I was glad of that. It was better not to hear what he had to say to me.

I felt awkward being alone in Mr. McNeal's living room with Jed, the cause of all the trouble. It was an honor to be invited into Mr. McNeal's home, but the reason I was here, of course, was shameful indeed. After all those decades of tranquility, I was a part of the era that had failed to uphold our end of the deal with Mr. McNeal.

I half expected that Mr. McNeal would take my life that night along with Jed's and I wouldn't have tried to stop him if he did. After all, we did fail him. It was our duty to restore the peace.

When Mr. McNeal returned, bearing a silver tray with my tea and a bowl of sugar, he offered me a reassuring smile. He apologized that there was no cream, but, as he explained, he rarely had guests who drank it and so it went bad rather quickly.

I pondered over that last statement. Were there other vampires like Mr. McNeal living in neighboring towns who came to visit him from time to time? Did he, or could he have such things as relatives? I wanted to ask him so badly, but I was in no position to interrogate him.

He was an extremely polite host. He did not begin to drink his beverage until I had completely finished mine. During that time, we engaged in small talk. It was a rather pleasant time, despite the circumstances, but for the life of me I cannot remember exactly what it was that we talked about. I can only remember that I had actually been enjoying myself and completely forgot that Jed was sitting there with us.

When I finished my tea, he offered me more, but I politely refused. He smiled and then looked longingly over at Jed.

Jed's eyes widened and he attempted to leap from the sofa, but Mr. McNeal's hand shot out and held him back. He moved so fast that I'm still not sure Jed had actually tried to flee at all.

Then Mr. McNeal shifted closer to Jed, calmly reached over and snapped his neck. He quickly opened a vein on Jed's neck with a fingernail and placed his mouth there to catch the flowing blood.

I was very surprised, of course, but also honored. Nobody that I'd known or heard of had ever observed Mr. McNeal drinking blood. I'd always thought that the Donated would still be alive and that the vampire would sink his teeth into their neck like in all those vampire movies. But instead, Mr. McNeal drank the blood from Jed's neck the way someone would put their lips around a water fountain.

I listened to the noises of the feast in amazement. There was nothing scary or painful about the experience like we had always thought. The legends had described the Donated as writhing in pain while their lifeblood was sucked from them. But this was nothing like those tales. Certainly, Mr. McNeal was drinking blood from a human's neck. But he was doing it in a dignified and distinguished manner, the way Queen Elizabeth might drink her tea.

When he finished, his lips were coated in deep crimson. He plucked a cloth napkin from the silver tray and diligently wiped the blood away. He then thanked me for the offering, and we agreed that such a thing was an unpleasant necessity. It should never happen again. Nor would it, I suggested, for we had learned our lesson. Now that we'd had a fitting punishment, actions such as Jed's would be very unlikely.

He led me to the door and bid me a fair evening.

Then, as if reading my mind as I stepped outside, he passed me a tissue from his inside breast pocket. I used it to dab at the tears which suddenly began to flow.

As he closed the door the spell I had been under faded even more. Grief flooded over my soul. I walked down his sidewalk, again past the lawn where those unfortunate children had once played, and the event I had just witnessed took effect.

I had sat there, with not a single protest to make, as a vampire killed and consumed the blood of my only son. Not only had I concurred with the event, but I had observed it without any emotion, as if I were a scientist recording data from a routine experiment.

And why?

Because I was under some sort of spell?

Perhaps. But I believe it was also because I was part of the example being set for the better of our entire town. Now that the example existed, parents would take the role of instructing their children in the importance of tradition more seriously. I had obviously failed somewhere down the line.

I had lost two people I loved to *The Ritual of the Drawing* and the traditions and customs which surrounded it. Seventeen years ago, my husband had sunk deeper into his drinking problem than ever before. Wandering the streets all hours of the night in a drunken manner, Earl had spent the better part of a year in the "drunk tank." He was no longer there for me or our baby. He neglected his job. His alcoholism got worse and worse as the days passed, until finally the elders decided that he was no longer of any use to society and was slated as one of the next year's Donated.

So, I had been forced to bring up Jed by myself. That wasn't easy, living in the shame of my husband. And I don't think I can use it as any excuse. If there's one thing I've learned living in Birks Falls, there's no such thing as a good excuse to shirk your civic duties. So, I failed as both a wife and a mother.

Perhaps parents will use my example for generations to come to teach their children the importance of personal responsibility, mutual trust and community chores. Hopefully, they will learn the reason why tradition is sacred and ultimately what happens when you shirk both your duties and tradition for some smaller personal cause.

Hopefully.

Only time will tell.

For now, though the streets are still safe, the unwanted dregs of society are not a threat to our peaceful haven. So long as we have Mr. McNeal and *The Ritual of the Drawing*.

Prospero's Ghost

Co-written with Kimberly Foottit

McMaster University - 1964

DR. MARSHALL EMERSON lost his balance as a student brushed past him in the stairwell, almost knocking the withered, leather-bound text out of his hand. Clutching the book to his chest, Emerson fell to one knee, sending a sharp pain up his side. With a grunt of annoyance, he checked the precious book to make sure it had not been damaged; he would sooner fall down the stairs than let it come to any harm.

"Sorry Professor Prospero," the youth said over his shoulder as he vaulted up the stairs. "I'm late for class."

"Rapscallion!" Emerson watched the youngster with the t-shirt and bell-bottom pants disappear through the doorway to the main floor of the library.

"Always rushing. Never pausing for deep thought or study."

Still on one knee, Emerson looked at the collection of Shakespeare's plays in his hand. The pain in his bones receded quickly when his eyes rested on the rare tome.

This single volume of Shakespeare's plays represented much of his life's work and focus. And though he thought his simple alliterative nickname was immature, he allowed a small part of him to warm with pride whenever he heard it.

"Professor Prospero, indeed," he said, shaking his head and briefly allowing a smile to cross his lips.

The stairwell door opened again, and the smile left as fast as it had appeared as a library assistant, this one dressed properly for an academic setting, rushed to help him. "Dr. Emerson," she said. "Are you okay? Let me help you up."

McMaster University - Present Day

Richard Hamill pulled the text from the display shelf, closing and locking the glass case. He turned the book over in his gloved hand, caressing the withered leather cover.

"I'm amazed at how well this has stood the test of time," he said to the young blond man beside him.

"Look at how solid and sturdy the spine and binding still are."

"It seems the perfect candidate for the Kirtas scanner," the young man, Matthew Phillips, said, reaching for the book.

Richard held the text away from his reach. "Your gloves," he insisted.

While he watched Matthew put them on, Richard said, "This particular book was owned by none other than the world-renowned Shakespearean scholar, Dr. Marshall P. Emerson.

"It's an 1861 reprint of the first folio edition of Shakespeare's plays and could easily fetch enough money to completely re-equip the William Ready Division of Archives and Research Collection here at McMaster."

"Wow. Really?"

"Absolutely. But I'd sooner die than see this book lost or sold, which is why I'm delighted we have the ability to scan and create a digital replication of it from which print on demand versions can be made."

"It allows others the ability to appreciate the text without having to handle the original," Matthew added.

"Exactly." Richard was always surprised at how the reverence for the printed word remained intact in someone so young during such technologically advanced times. "These archives aren't about the monetary value of the texts, but more about the cultural significance," the older man added.

And this one held plenty.

"On top of its standing as the first reliable printing of twenty of Shakespeare's plays in 1623, this book is held in regard from its final ownership by McMaster's own Dr. Emerson," Richard continued.

"Professor Prospero," Matthew grinned, unable to hold back and wanting to display his knowledge. "The leading expert on *The Tempest* for over thirty years, and controversial in his proclamation that it was an example of one of Shakespeare's finest tragedies, despite the more popular supposition of the play being a comedy."

"Indeed he was," Richard said, bemused at how Matthew sounded as though he were reciting the facts straight from Wikipedia.

"Did you ever meet him?" the young man asked.

"No. I joined the university six years after he died."

"So, you never witnessed if the rumors were true."

"The rumors?" Richard said, fighting the shiver crawling up his spine.

"That he carried this book with him no matter where he went."

Richard relaxed. "Oh, that. Yes. Yes, apparently, it's true. He was said to be a difficult man, not love by his colleagues; yet when he passed on, his entire collection of books, including the much-adored text he always carried around campus was bequeathed to the library archives."

"And," Matthew said, his eyes brimming with curiosity, "what about the *other* rumors?"

Richard felt his shoulders tense again. "What *other* rumors?"

"The legend of Prospero's Ghost."

He averted his eyes from the young man. "Hogwash."

"Really? I've heard that the ghost of Dr. Emerson has been seen wandering the library halls endlessly searching for his lost book. You mean you've never seen him?"

"No," Richard said, his eyes not returning to his assistant. "No. Never. Those are just silly stories."

McMaster University – 1970

On his first week of work at McMaster, Richard Hamill not only saw a ghost for the very first time in his life, but he heard it, too.

Hamill was making the rounds on a Thursday night, ensuring the top floor of the library was cleared and that any books left in the study carrels were placed on the "to be shelved" carts in the main aisle. Though it was his first week, he'd become fond of the late shift and the wonderful quiet and solitude that came at the end of a long and busy day.

As he was passing an aisle he thought he saw someone out of the corner of his eye, just off to the left. It appeared to be an older man with grey hair in a dark jacket crouching to look at the books on the shelf second from the bottom.

Hamill turned on his heel and headed down the aisle prepared to politely ask the patron to retrieve their books and proceed to the checkout downstairs.

But there was nobody there.

He took a few steps forward to stand in front of the shelves where he thought he'd seen the figure crouching.

This was the drama section. The second shelf from the bottom held Shakespeare's works. Hamill had been in the section not two hours earlier, having resorted the previously unordered books.

But they were strewn about again. A complete mess, as if a child had been searching for something and been unable to find it.

He was furious. He was certain the figure he had seen had messed up the books. Dashing down the aisle, he looked left, then right.

On the periphery of his vision, a scrawny grey-haired figure shuffled by on his left, quickly disappearing behind the shelves of the aisle he'd just been in.

"Excuse me!" Hamill said, racing in that direction, unashamed of the loudness of his voice in such a quiet place.

But, as before, when he got to the end of that aisle, nobody was there.

He looked left and right.

The stacks were quiet and still.

Then, just as he was about to head back to the mess and tidy it for the second time that night, he heard a distinct low voice echo across the library, coming from the drama aisle he'd just vacated.

"All . . . all lost, quite lost . . ."

The voice faded in and out like a radio tuned to a strange station from another world. At the same time the words reached his ears, a cool chill, not unlike a stiff fall breeze, settled over him.

But in the same manner the words faded, so too did the chill, leaving Richard Hamill alone in the library to mark that day, April 23rd, as the start of what would later become a life-long passion of studying Dr. Marshall P. Emerson.

McMaster University – Present Day

Placing the book carefully on the Kirtas APT 2400 scanner, Matthew reached up to adjust the focus of the top left camera.

While disappointed that Dr. Hamill hadn't stayed with him, as he had more questions and enjoyed listening to tales about the university's history from his mentor, he also found joy in the solitude offered by his role. Slipping the ear buds back on, he pressed play on his mp3 player and then adjusted the attachments that would hold the pages flat while they were scanned.

As Matthew turned toward the keyboard to enter specifications into the software that ran the machine, he didn't hear the creak of the door opening behind him.

He'd just entered the keystrokes to begin the process that would capture a digital image of each page, then carefully turn the pages until the entire book was photographed—a process that took no more than about fifteen minutes—when a shadow fell over him.

Matthew turned to see who was there.

☠   ☠   ☠

It had been a long day at the library. Nancy Irving, rubbing the back of her neck with a tired hand, headed into the special collections section. Students could be so demanding some days. There was just one more book to return before finally calling it a day.

As she passed by the scan room, she noticed the light was on. Knowing Dr. Hamill was in his office, she could only assume that Matthew Phillips was still in there, tinkering around with the library's new toy. She stopped and checked her watch. It was well past Matthew's finishing time. She sighed. For such a bright boy, he could be so absentminded. If it wasn't his pass card, it was his water bottle or his glasses. Now it seemed his forgetfulness had moved onto leaving the lights on.

When Nancy entered the room, the machine was humming. She frowned as she noticed that the book still in the machine was quite old. This had to be more than just carelessness on Matthew's part. Dr. Hamill spoke so highly of him, and she had personally seen the boy with the books. He was always so careful.

She was about to reach for the mouse, to turn off the screen saver and start the shutdown process when the figure in the corner caught her attention.

The young man was pushed into the corner, as though backing away from something until the walls had stopped his progress. The body was pale and rigid, but it was the look of sheer terror on Matthew Phillips' face that froze the scream building in Nancy Irving's throat.

He was dead.

Yet still standing – rigid, like a stone statue.

Dr. Richard Hamill ignored the carriage clock on his bookshelf as it chimed the late hour. Without family to go home to, his office had been his refuge after many a trying day, but there was no peace tonight.

He stared into the amber liquid that swirled in the short square glass in his hand. It was usually a calming movement, meant to still the mind, but instead it just brought up more questions.

The police had long removed the body of poor Matthew Phillips and were now finishing up their crime scene investigation. He should be down there, making sure they didn't damage any of the precious and fragile editions that lay in the collection, but he couldn't bring himself to enter those rooms. Not yet.

Nancy Irving had been given a strong sedative and taken home by her sister who worked in the campus bookstore. Of all the people in the library, it would have to be the most sensitive and kindly of women to find a body. Had it been Mora Collins, the slightly gothic intern in the map room, perhaps there wouldn't have been quite the kerfuffle. Richard sighed. With Nancy's dramatics, it was guaranteed that the entire campus would know the elaborate version of the grisly discovery before the morning papers hit the doorsteps.

But it wasn't the bad press Richard Hamill feared. It wasn't the badgering of the campus and city police that pushed him to pull out his secret bottle from the bottom drawer of his desk and seek solace in its amber glow.

It was that book.

Professor Emerson's book of Shakespeare. That was the volume found in the machine by Nancy Irving before she turned and saw Matthew's horrified face. The computer had long since completed its scan before the young man was discovered. The information now waited for transfer to the bookstore so the book could be printed out on their new-fangled book machine.

Professor Prospero's favorite volume. The jewel of his collection.

Richard took a swig of his drink, closing his eyes as it coated the heavy spot in his belly with a layer of warmth. But it didn't penetrate the feeling; the dread that had started growing there ever since Matthew had expressed an interest in the book's history.

Prospero had loved that book so, and now it seemed he had come back to reclaim it.

Richard raised his glass to the dim light around him.

"Welcome home, Marshall. Welcome home."

McMaster University – 1964

Alistair Rogers straightened his tie for the umpteenth time while he waited for Dr. Emerson –

his two o'clock appointment. He wasn't sure why, but Professor Prospero had always intimidated him. It was laughable really, a man as old and frail as Emerson making him feel like he was a naughty schoolboy. The two men had started off on the wrong foot when the librarian had foolishly asked to touch the professor's precious volume of Shakespeare. The affront had carried through their relationship no matter how accommodating or ingratiating Rogers had tried to be.

That was about to change. He was sure of it.

Then there was a knock at his door and the eminent Professor was before him.

"Dr. Emerson," Rogers stood and came around his desk, hand outstretched. "I'm so happy you could meet me today."

"*Mr.* Rogers," the older man greeted, emphasizing the mister in his usual disdainful tone. He put out his hand and allowed it to be shook, but it was clear that it was a polite social gesture only.

Rogers chose to ignore the attitude and waved a hand to the empty chair in front of his desk. "Please sir, have a seat."

Emerson sat with a rickety grace, putting his worn leather briefcase on the floor with delicate care.

"Well Professor, I'll get right to the point," Rogers began, settling into his own chair. "As you may have heard the library has just acquired the new Xerox

2400. It's the latest in high volume copying technology. We now have the ability to preserve some of our oldest texts so we don't have to handle the originals and can make them available to a much wider student base for research purposes. We would be most honored if we could borrow your volume of Shakespeare's works for the inaugural copy."

Rogers took a breath, waiting for the pleased, perhaps flattered, reaction to his proposal.

The silence was long as Emerson's face turned a deep hue of scarlet.

"I was unaware this institution was supporting mass copyright infringement," Professor Emerson finally replied, his tone cold, almost horrified. Reflexively, he reached for the briefcase, bringing it to his lap.

Rogers noticed the movement and guessed the edition in question was within its depths. "It's Shakespeare, sir. His work is in the public domain. It belongs to the world now and is not restricted by modern copyright laws. None of the classics are." The librarian noted Emerson's hold on the briefcase, the wringing of the bag's straps under gnarled white knuckles. "I assure you; no harm will come to the book."

Emerson rose, clutching the bag to his chest. "It is not merely a *book*, Mr. Rogers. This edition is a precious treasure. I certainly wouldn't expect you to comprehend its value."

Rogers stood as well. This was not going well, and he had, yet again, offended the sensitive man. "But surely, Professor Emerson, you recognize the significance of making such a classic available to everyone."

"Such classic, unique editions should *not* be available to everyone!" Emerson turned to leave.

"With all due respect sir, Shakespeare wrote for the masses. It would be a shame to deny this generation such a treasure."

The professor turned back. "Shakespeare wrote for royalty, Mr. Rogers. And the masses of Elizabethan England were far more civilized and worthy of such art than the barbarous hordes of today with their long hair and loose clothing and rock and roll. Good day sir!"

The slamming of the door behind him punctuated his departure.

Rogers sighed as he sat back in his chair. His colleagues had laughed at him when he had made the suggestion at the last board meeting. They warned him against approaching the crotchety old eccentric, especially about anything regarding his precious volume of Shakespeare. He hated hearing "I told you so." Rumor had it that the old man was nearing retirement. Picking up the receiver of his phone and dialing the extension number of Frank

Letts, the board chair, Rogers thought that day couldn't come soon enough.

McMaster University - Present Day

Alan Lester moved the mouse, manipulating the icon on the screen and clicking the button to start the next print job. He looked at his watch as the Espresso Book Machine started spitting out printed pages into the collector tray. Titles bookstore had been closed for a couple of hours and he was just over half done the order. All the drama at the library had delayed the transfer of the file, making him pull a late shift to get the copies needed for the students.

He sighed. That poor kid. He couldn't even begin to imagine what the parents must be going through. Didn't want to. Right now, his own son would be out of the tub, a nightly pre-bedtime bath before heading off to visit the sandman. It was the best part of the day for Alan. Stretched out on the bed, his young son curled up under the covers, sharing a story or two. He couldn't imagine not ever doing that again.

The printer stopped and the carriage hummed to life, ready for the next step in the printing process.

Alan checked his watch again. With over half the order of the book already waiting in receiving, maybe he would get out a couple more copies and then call it a night. It wouldn't be the entire order, but he could easily come in early and print off the rest. Students never came into the store first thing in the morning anyway.

He was just about to write a note to Patricia Irving, explaining the missing texts, when he heard the distinct sound of shuffling through the book stacks. He frowned, paused in his movement, listened for the sound again. When nothing came, he shrugged it off. He knew he was in the store alone. Had been for hours.

He picked up the pen again, and heard the noise, this time closer.

"Hello?" he called out, turning from the machine, pen still in hand.

No reply. No noise.

He chuckled at his own ridiculous behavior. He really had to stop reading those horror novels before bed. He stopped when the noise came again.

This time, he didn't call out, but moved, walking slowly towards the sound.

Alan turned the corner, struck by the sight of an older man, slim and gangly looking in his grey trousers and dark tweed blazer.

"Excuse me sir, how did you get in here?" Alan asked, surprised at the steadiness of his own voice despite the rapid thudding of his heart.

The man turned, revealing a haughty facial expression dominated by dark blazing eyes behind silver rimmed glasses.

"He that dies, pays all debts," he said in an even voice.

Alan frowned. "Sir?" he asked. "Do you know where you are?"

"In the company of the Bard," came the reply.

The bookstore employee looked at the sign above the closest bookshelf and realized they were indeed standing in the Shakespeare section of the store.

He thought about it. While the store was cleared out by the closing staff, it was entirely possible for them to have missed one person, quietly loitering in an out of the way section such as this. Hidden away among the stacks, the poor man could have been locked in all night.

"We've been closed for quite some time, sir. Is there someone I can call to come and get you?"

"Hell is empty, and all the devils are here."

Alan frowned again. It was obvious the man was quoting Shakespeare, but he couldn't remember which one of the plays the words came from. Despite his theatre background, the Bard had never been his strong suit.

Deep in thought, he didn't notice the older man's approach until he was close enough to touch. Alan started, dropping his pen on the floor, suddenly frozen with the chill of the air around him.

The man bent down with a rickety grace. Where he would have brushed the younger man's legs, there was only a cool breeze. He was speaking as he rose up.

"You taught me language; and my profit on't is I know how to curse . . ."

Alan, wide eyed and shocked, groped blindly for the source of the pain in his neck. His hand rested on his pen, thrust into his throat by a man that seemed like he had barely enough strength to stand. He tried to pull it out, but the flow of blood was too swift, and he felt the power and will drain from his own body. He slid to the floor, his last sight and sound coming from the old man, his figure shimmering with his last words.

". . . the red plague rid you for learning me your language."

Patricia Irving yawned as she pushed the big blue cart laden with texts down the deserted hallway. Despite the fact that she wasn't a morning person, she had to admit to herself that this was the best part of her day. The university was largely deserted at eight am, only the occasional groggy student shuffling to class met her in the hall.

She reached for the Tim Horton's cup on the cart, taking a careful sip as she walked. Usually that was all she needed – a coffee and a cigarette to face the day. This morning was different, however, having just finished her fourth cigarette and was now on her third extra large double-double. Her husband would have a fit if he knew, but luckily she had left him to watch Nancy and drove herself into work that morning. What he didn't know wouldn't kill him.

She cringed at her involuntary choice of words. Poor Nancy. Normally her sister was someone who had a flair for melodrama, but last night her inconsolable fear and grief was genuine after finding that unfortunate Phillips boy. Patricia loved books, especially a good thriller, but after having heard the details of an incident so close to home in all their chilling glory, she was looking forward to shelving the business books rattling on her cart.

The elevator's final stop boomed, echoing into the high ceilings of the auxiliary bookstore commonly referred to as The Tank. It was a large space in the sub-basement of one of the Arts buildings, once a water reservoir before the bookstore took possession of it in the late seventies. Cold and sterile, it had become Patricia's second home since she became textbook buyer in the early eighties. It was humid in the summer and cold in the winter, murals of sea life painted on the walls making it no less gloomy. Dust bunnies conspired in every corner and the fluorescent lights hummed overhead constantly. Still she loved it at this time of the day. Quiet and deserted, with only half the lights lit.

She left the lights as they were, knowing the cashier would turn them all on when she came down in a half an hour and another sales day would begin. Until then it would be her and the books, exactly the way she liked it.

Patricia flicked on the radio as she put her purse and coffee down on the text desk at the back of the store. Coffee alone wasn't going to keep her awake this morning after a night of soothing her excitable sister. The station sputtered through static before the tinny refrain of a song came through the speakers. It was the oldies station and Patricia smiled and hummed along as the music took her back to her youth.

In this manner, the business books came off the cart in no time. Accessing the computer, Patricia punched in the ISBN of the smaller paperback stacked on the bottom shelf of the cart. She frowned when she realized it was a Print On Demand book ordered for a course and half that order was missing.

After a futile search for a note of explanation, Patricia stood, trying to recall if she saw something on the floor in receiving. She sighed, remembering nothing and silently kicked herself for not making a stop at the EBM desk before picking up the cart and heading to the tank. The books were already being asked for by students eager to begin their studies, so Patricia pushed the cart to the appropriate shelf, making a mental note to send those students who didn't get a copy fast enough to Alan Lester. Let the store's Book Manager take the complaints.

As she maneuvered the cart between the high metal shelves filled with texts, the air seemed to chill. Patricia shivered, frowning as she pushed. It was only early October and while there was an autumn nip in the air that morning, it shouldn't be this cold, even in the sub-basement.

Methodically, she began to stack the books on the appropriate shelf, trying to convince herself that the air wasn't getting colder with every text. When the last copy was in her hands, she looked down, her frown deepening as she read the cover. It was a folio edition of the works of Shakespeare.

From 1861.

The frown slid from her face as a picture of the original cover popped into her head. A book, worn and withered, grasped in the gnarled fingers of old hands, shoved into her face over forty years before. She remembered the day quite clearly, one of her first as a part time general books employee at the bookstore. She was as green as they come then, full of a passion for books. She never dreamed that she would make a career out of her part time job, and while she didn't regret her decision to stay, that one day had almost pushed her to the door. That wretched old man.

And that book.

The lights flickered, and the chill in the air grew as Patricia Irving stood frozen to the spot, still holding the book.

She never noticed the pale hand reach out for her shoulder.

"Morning, Pat," the cashier said, jumping a little and giggling when the older woman started. "Sorry, I didn't mean to scare you."

Patricia forced a smile, the lights on full and the chill in the air gone. "Good morning, Rose. You didn't scare me."

The young woman gave her a strange look. "Are you alright?" she asked.

"Yes. Yes. Just too much coffee this morning."

The cashier smiled and walked back to the front of the store, leaving Patricia at the bookshelf.

"No dear," she said quietly, shelving the remaining text. "*You* didn't scare me at all."

McMaster University – 1964

Patricia Irving nervously pushed the cart out from the receiving area onto the brightly lit floor of the new bookstore. Having recently moved into the basement of the newest building on campus, the selection of general books had expanded, opening up part time positions in that department. Patricia, a part-time student cashier, now finishing her second year at McMaster, had been given a chance to prove herself by being offered a position on the general books team.

A lover of fiction, she was delighted with the opportunity to showcase her knowledge of both the classics as well as modern writers.

The bright wooden cart, filled with paperbacks from Pan and Penguin, vibrated due to a wobbly front wheel. Patricia frowned and bent low to examine the wheel as she kept moving forward.

The cart bumped into something soft.

"My word," a gruff voice sounded, and Patricia looked up at a dark eyed man with white hair that she immediately recognized as the professor for her class on Victorian literature.

"Can't you watch where you're going with that thing?" he asked.

"Sorry, Dr. Emerson," she said in a low voice.

His dark eyes fell on the cart of books and he let out a loud harrumph. "So, this is what passes for literature today, is it? Mass produced pocket books manufactured like so much candy for the mind."

Believing she could impress him, Patricia held up the Pan books new release of Ian Fleming's latest novel, *On Her Majesty's Secret Service*. "Oh but, sir, this is such a wonderful novel, an utterly compelling read. I couldn't afford the hardback edition – but here it is, a compact, low cost option. Fleming is the master of the spy thriller."

Emerson let out a slow sigh as he glanced at the art on the cover. "A ring in a field of bloody snow? I fail to see how that can be a *wonderful novel*.

"The bard was the master of suspense and intrigue. He wrote tales from the richness of history, characters that live and breathe in the minds of readers today. Not like this Fleming hack and his forgettable *Bond* character."

Patricia placed the book back on the cart, her face turning red and her eyes downcast.

"What other *treasures* does your cart hold?"

Feeling she might be able to redeem herself in the professor's eyes she remembered the series of Shakespeare's plays on the other side of the cart. She ran her hand along the spines until she found a copy of *The Tempest*. She pulled it out and held it to show him.

"Isn't this beautiful?" she said in a hopeful voice.

The professor was silent as he stared at the book.

Carefully, he leaned forward, plucked the book from her hand using the tips of his fingers, as if it were covered in mold or slime and flung it across the floor. Then he fixed his eyes on her.

"You mock me!" he growled. "Shakespeare was not meant to be published in such a low-quality mass-produced format."

"But sir . . ."

Emerson thrust the leather-bound Shakespeare book in her face, producing it from thin air.

"This!" he yelled. "*This* is fine literature. *This* is the way it was meant to be presented." He shook the book in her face. Despite the copy almost blocking her face, she could still feel drops of spittle from his lips land on her cheek.

"Shakespeare was never, *never*, meant to be lowered to this sort of mass production."

He slammed the fist of his free hand down on the cart, shaking his head, his face and neck turning a dark crimson.

"Why, oh why must this bookstore, this *campus* mock me?!"

He pushed at the uneven cart, the faulty wheel giving way. The cart tipped over on its side with a loud crash, spilling paperbacks across the tile floor as Emerson stormed out.

"Bloody stupid bookstore," he called out. "You'll not see me dare set foot in here again!"

Patricia stared at the books on the floor and began to cry.

McMaster University - 1973

Richard Hamill hadn't entered the library on an April 23rd since that first strange occurrence three years earlier. He'd always feigned illness or booked that week off work, whatever it took to ensure he wasn't around.

He knew enough to have determined that the specter he'd seen on the top floor of the library that April night in 1970 was that of Professor Marshall Emerson, Shakespearean scholar. There were enough clues and Hamill was a competent enough researcher to be able to home in on the quote from *The Tempest* he'd heard the ghost utter, the significance of the date and the section of the library that had been disturbed.

But it wasn't any of the research or clues he'd put together that made him confident in his decision.

It was that portrait in the archives section of the library, down in the depths of the basement which he'd spotted the next day that clinched it. All those other clues were mere window dressing.

He barely glanced at the portrait when he walked past the first time. It was hung above a cubicle leading to the back of the archives – but a second after he passed it, he stopped, and the peripheral glance of the man in the photograph was enough to set all his hairs on end and give him a sinking feeling in his gut.

When he stepped back to look directly at the photo of Marshall Emerson he knew immediately. *That* had been the man he'd seen the night before on the top floor of the library; a man who had been dead for years.

Richard knew enough not to mention his suspicion to anyone. But he'd kept his ears open for any disturbing stories or tales and jotted down anything that was even slightly out of the ordinary, just in case it had something to do with Emerson's ghost.

He kept his notes on these matters as well as the tons of research he had done on the man's life in a secret file that he simply labeled *Prospero's Ghost*.

And he was working on a note within that file on the second night he'd witnessed the apparition. He'd been sitting in the cubicle below Emerson's portrait, a cubicle he'd become rather fond of over the years despite that heavy feeling in his gut he experienced when he'd first seen it.

As he was making a quick note about a part-time student who had reported the Shakespeare collection on the top floor having been found strewn about the floor when a distinct chill encompassed the room.

Out of the corner of his eye, Richard saw a figure standing before him. When he glanced up, nobody was there, but he heard, very clearly, the following words in a gruff deep voice: "Knowing I loved my books, he furnished me from mine own library with volumes that I prize above my dukedom."

Richard paused only a moment before responding, almost by rote, since he immediately recognized the line as one the character Prospero said in Act I Scene ii of *The Tempest*. Once he started studying Marshall Emerson, he, in turn, studied the bard's works in detail, particularly that one play – the swan song of Shakespeare and apparently Emerson as well.

"Would I might but ever see that man!"

The response from the gruff voice was immediate. "Sit still and hear the last of our sea sorrow."

The chill immediately withdrew from the room and Richard was alone again.

He didn't have to make a note about this newly discovered fact.

Marshall could be pacified with the right words, the right response. Now he only needed to discover what the right response would be to rid the library of Prospero's Ghost forever.

McMaster University - Present Day

Titles bookstore had only been open for about an hour and was still quiet when Richard rushed over to the Espresso Book Machine at the back of the sales floor. Ten minutes earlier, having returned to the Kirtas scanner room, Richard saw on the library's computer system that the Emerson Shakespeare folio had been uploaded to the bookstore's server.

Having been a regular customer for years, Richard was known to many of the full-time staff at the store, including Melinda Harvey who was manning the customer service desk that day. He made small talk with the young woman, mentioning an order he had placed with the EBM staff. Might he have a look to see if it was completed? Melinda had seen the librarian plenty of times with Alan Lester and Patricia Irving, playing with the new machine. She smiled and waved him by her desk.

Richard had observed Alan and Patricia enough to know the basics of how the machine operated. He quickly tabbed through the interface screens to see that the title had been added and had indeed been printed. Fifty-six copies to be exact. The print queue still had forty-four lined up to print.

The last copy had been printed at 9:20 PM.

Walking around the back of the machine to see if the books were anywhere nearby, he spotted Alan Lester's body slumped behind the Espresso Book Machine on a pile of paper boxes, a pen sticking out of his throat.

The young man lay face down, almost as though he had been dumped behind the machine so as not to be found. There wasn't a single drop of blood from his wound, yet Richard knew before he bent over to check for a pulse that the man was dead. Prospero had struck again.

He sighed as he looked down at the body. Alan had been a good friend. He was young, had a full life ahead of him. Richard offered a silent prayer and took a deep breath, trying to steady his nerves and slow the pounding of his heart as he turned away.

He knew that nothing could save the book manager now, and it would be useless to create a panic. It was with a surprisingly calm voice that he asked Melinda to call security. Her questioning glance was stilled by his stricken face, but when security picked up, she put her hand over the mouthpiece of the phone, and asked:

"What should I say is the reason?"

"Tell them Alan Lester is dead. They need to come to the store now."

Her look of shock and fear made him step forward, put a slightly shaking hand on her arm.

"Now is not the time to panic, my dear. Just stay calm and wait for security."

He didn't wait for her response as he headed to the back entrance of the store, walking as quickly as possible without attracting attention. It was obvious to him that if the books weren't in the store, they had to have already been taken to The Tank. He knew the staff well, especially his good friend Patricia Irving. She would know where the copies were. As he cleared the store and began to run through the halls, he only hoped he wasn't too late.

☠   ☠   ☠

One of the benefits of having worked with someone for over 30 years was the inherent trust that allowed for communication short-cuts to be employed. When Richard found Patricia in The Tank, it didn't take much to convince her what was going on, and despite the bizarre nature of his explanation, she immediately believed him.

Pulling the copies of the book off the shelf for English 3K06 they threw them onto a cart.

"Should we burn these copies?" Patricia asked. "Will that put his spirit to rest?"

"Probably," Richard nodded, then grinned and started to chuckle.

"What?" Patricia asked.

"In all the years we've known each other and shared our mutual passion for books, did you *ever* think one of us would suggest burning books as a good idea?"

A nervous giggle escaped from Patricia's throat. She had to admit, it felt good.

"I'd have said hell would have to freeze over first before I ever considered it."

"No kidding."

"Okay, I have twenty-four copies here. How many did you pull off?"

"Thirty-one."

They exchanged a dark look.

"There's one missing."

A low howl began to rise up from the back corner of The Tank. With nary a window or even glimpse of the outdoors, a cold wind blew down the aisles of the store as if it were in the middle of an open field.

"No," Richard said, running toward the front of the room with one of the books in his hand.

He reached the cash registers where Rose was serving a student. Richard pushed himself between the customer and the cashier, holding up the book.

"Did you sell a copy of this book this morning?"

Rose threw a confused look at Patricia who nodded, letting her know that Richard was not a threat despite the mad look in his eyes. The young woman took another look at the book. "No," she replied. "I haven't."

Richard turned back to Patricia.

"So where is it?"

The howling wind intensified. Papers and register slips near the cash register begin to swirl into the air.

"W-what's going on?" Rose yelled, as she and her customer began batting at the pages swirling around their heads. A few of them seemed to have nicked at their skin.

The flying pages nearest Richard sliced at his bare skin as well; dozens of paper cuts striking him at lightning fast speed.

The tempestuous winds raged louder as he ducked and tried to ward off the paper cuts. His hands and face were turning into a road-map of cuts. Barely distinguishable within the howling screams of the wind and the others in The Tank, Richard was able to pick out a gruff voice. "I will plague them all, even to roaring!"

From the far aisle, a student with a large backpack who Richard hadn't seen earlier bolted toward the metal stairs leading to the exit. He ran through the security gates, triggering the alarm with his passing, and leapt up the stairs. The heavy fire door at the top slammed shut with a thunderous bang just before he reached it. He pushed on the door's panic bar, but it wouldn't open.

"Hey!" Richard ran up the stairs with a surprising agility for a man his age and tore the backpack from the student's shoulder. He opened it, revealing three shoplifted textbooks, one of which was the replica version of Emerson's prized Shakespeare folio.

He held the book up as the pages continued to strike at his skin. He did his best to ignore the pain screaming to him from dozens of tiny cuts.

"This is the last one, Marshall!" he yelled into the storm. "No more blasphemous replicas of your text will be made. The offending bastard offspring will all be destroyed. This I vow to you." The flying papers continued to strike at his exposed flesh and the wind increased in intensity; enough to start lifting textbooks off the adjacent shelves and into a rising whirlwind.

Patricia, Rose and the student at the cash desk all scrambled for cover.

Still standing at the top of the metal staircase, Richard held the book opened at the midpoint, tiny trails of blood from his palms streaming onto the pages of the book. He grunted as he tore it in two. Several of the swirling textbooks slammed into his chest, shoulders and head, and he dropped the pieces as he stumbled to his knees halfway down the metal staircase.

"Marshall!" Richard screamed, holding onto the railing to keep from falling further. "I long to hear the story of your life!"

The wind immediately stopped.

The swirling books plummeted to the floor.

In the fresh quiet a gruff voice echoed from the far corner of The Tank. "I'll deliver all and promise you calm seas."

Richard got to his feet and walked down the stairs to stand beside Patricia as the papers that had been striking at them floated gently down to the ground.

As he reached her, more words could be heard, loud and distinct at first, but slowly fading.

"Now my charms are all o'erthrown . . ."

"It's over?" Patricia asked.

Richard nodded. "It's over. The final act." He took Patricia's hand in his own. "Rest in peace, Marshall. Be free and fair thou well."

University of Alberta – Present Day

"What's coming off the machine now?" Andy Todd, the bookstore director said as he walked into the lower level area where the University's Espresso Book Machine was located.

Laura Ryan smiled at him, not able to hear him over the sound of the hydraulic pump of the trimmer, but pretty sure she knew what he'd asked.

"It's a new file I just pulled off the EBM master server. It looks like Alan over at McMaster uploaded it late last night."

"Is it another one of their library archives texts?" Andy asked, rounding the corner to have a closer look. The trimming process completed, and the louder noise stopped.

"Yeah. A rare original printing of Shakespeare's complete works." She grinned. Though she'd operated the machine for close to two years, every new title she produced on the EBM gave her a quick thrill. "The first one is just about to come out."

They watched the book drop down the chute and out of the machine. Laura picked it up and quickly fanned through the pages. "Looks good," she said.

"Excellent," Andy said. "Okay, I'm heading home. Don't work too late."

"I won't," Laura grinned.

As they exchanged pleasantries and Andy turned to leave, neither of them noticed the dark shadowy figure in a brown tweed jacket lurking behind the closest set of bookshelves.

Behind the Screams

I CONTINUE TO receive plenty of comments and emails from readers who tell me that they quite enjoy the "behind the story" notes that I add to many of my short stories and collections of short fiction.

And so, I present here, a few insights and some background information either on the inspiration or source for each of the stories you have just read.

If you're not a person who enjoys watching the special features on a DVD or the movie along with commentary from the actors or director, then I suggest you simply stop reading now. Thanks for picking up this collection and reading a few of my stories. I hope you enjoyed them enough to want to read more of my fiction.

If, however, you do enjoy that "behind the curtains" peek into my fiction, then we still have a little bit of time left in our "Ode to Classics." Let me share with you some further background and insights into the tales you just read.

About "Memento Mori"

Originally published in print in **Sulphur: Laurentian University's Literary Journal Volume III** *(March 2013), as well as online in* **Dissections: The Journal of Contemporary Horror**.

THE FIRST DRAFT of this story was written shortly after I had discovered the Mark Twain tale "A Curious Dream." Twain's story, which had originally been published in *The Buffalo Express* in the spring of 1870 was a social satire meant to expose the neglect of local cemeteries. The piece had apparently had an effect on Buffalo citizens and led to improvements being made as well as national reform.

I was fascinated by the manner in which Twain exposed, in a satirical fashion, the neglect of local cemeteries while poking fun at the materialism inherent in society as well as the social posturing and sense of entitlement that existed in his day. Perhaps I was so fascinated because I imagined, if Twain thought those issues were present then, I could only imagine how he might view them today.

I enjoyed the darkly humorous way in which Twain's tale unfolded. The narrator's bizarre encounter with one of the skeletons from a procession of emigrating dead stuck with me.

I marveled at a number of questions.

Witnessing such a thing, why would the narrator simply react so calmly? Was it because he knew, all along, that it was a dream – and indeed, in dreams don't we accept the bizarre and twisted in a matter-of-fact manner? But in any case, his nonplussed reaction in and of itself leant to the mystique to the tale.

The ending, I felt, was interesting, and served Twain's purpose effectively.

But I wanted to do more with it.

I wanted to imagine a slightly darker interpretation of what the dead might do when faced with such neglect of their resting place; and, like Twain, I wanted to inject my own nugget of a themed lesson. I wanted to poke fun at the procrastination that is inherent in our society, at the tendencies to either leave something for later or for someone else to take care of.

The tale rolled out nicely – after writing it, I had to go back and ensure that, while I wanted to follow the original tale's structure, pace and style, I needed it to have its own life and unique pulse. There was a desire to preserve the original language, but I ended up modernizing some of the phrases and expressions. I wanted the reader to immediately recognize that this was a play on Twain's original piece but divert from that story enough to make it my own.

In a nutshell, this was a fun story for me to write.

I particularly enjoyed trying to mimic, as much as possible, the voice and style of the original piece. That can often be a really fun challenge for a writer.

It took me much longer to come up with a title. I wanted, in the title, to elude to Twain's original story, so that it would be clear, even before reading, that my intent was to pay homage to Twain. *A Curious Nightmare* did that for me. But it wasn't enough. I went back to the tale, pulled out the Latin phrase "Memento Mori" and used that – but I kept a subtitle in order to ensure the element of Twain's original tale was immediately apparent.

About "The Ritual of the Drawing"

ONE THING I quite liked about Shirley Jackson's "The Lottery" is the manner by which people are going about in their every-day tradition, the horror bubbling just beneath the surface until the very end, when it all turns on one character.

Having grown up in a small town, I was familiar with the concept of ritual and how it can be an all-consuming element of the lives of the people who live there.

But in a bit of a diversion from the Jackson tale, I wanted to write a story in which you knew, right from the beginning, the horrific tradition of the town. That you knew *why* the town came to that agreement.

The "reveal" at the end was to be that the narrator herself was going through the process of committing the ultimate sacrifice of one of her own children. And that, even though she had some remorse over it, she manages to still push that aside for the "better" of society. It was, partially, a "generation gap" exploration, particularly with her expressing how the youth of today don't respect tradition, and I was trying to draw on that from similar arguments and bemoaning I had witnessed happening in the existing differences between my own younger generation and our elders.

Of course, when I first wrote that story I was in my early twenties. Imagining the mother, the main character, in her mid-forties was an intriguing concept for me. Now, as I write these notes, I realize that I'm actually now older than my un-named narrator. And I'm asking myself if I now feel the way I imagined she would feel about the younger generation – that there's a loss of respect for tradition, for responsibility. While I might have been seen yelling at young kids to get off my lawn (in the traditional of crabby older men everywhere), I can't say I think that specifically about the younger generation – but I *will* admit to thinking that about society in general. So, take from that what you will.

The location of Birks Falls came from a friend of mine from Carleton University. Christel grew up in Burks Falls, which is located about half-way between North Bay and Orillia on Highway 11 in Ontario. That particular village has less than 1,000 people in it, so I needed to fictionalize a place that "sounded" remote like Birks Falls, but had more people, but not too many. I grew up in Onaping Falls (comprised of the villages/townships of Levack, Onaping and Dowling) which had about 6,000 people. So I combined the population and elements of each of those locales and created the fictional Burks Falls. (Of course, memory might be failing me on that one. For all I know, I merely spelled Burks Falls incorrectly – but part of me remembers wanting the town to sound like a real place, but not BE that place because of the differences in population; not to mention, of course, the vampire, that, I'm pretty sure likely doesn't live in that town a few hours' drive south of North Bay.

About "Prospero's Ghost"

Originally published in **Campus Chills**, *2009*

THE CONCEPT FOR "Prospero's Ghost" was originally born on a University campus in the early 1990's when I was teaching drama at "Campus Camp" a summer program for 9 to 15-year-olds at Carleton University.

During a tour of Southam Hall's Alumni Theatre (now known at the Kailash Mital Theatre), I had the students sit on the dimly lit stage in a small pool of light while, standing just on the edge of the light, I told them the creepy story of how late one night I was in the theatre alone cleaning up when I encountered the ghost of the theatre, whom I nicknamed "Prospero's Ghost."

In my tale, the ghost was a construction worker who had been working on the building when it was first being built.

The man, a lover of Shakespeare, could often be found reading a pocket-book edition of *The Tempest* during his breaks, and was known for quoting the Bard when speaking to his fellow employees. And the well-worn copy of the play could often be seen sticking out of the back pocket of his jeans, since he never went anywhere without it.

One day, while working on the not-yet fully completed roof, he fell to his death on the concrete floor beneath the very stage where we were all standing. Witnesses to the event say that he died on the spot and that it was a surreal experience to be looking down from the roof above at his dead body lying on the cold concrete floor just inches away from the precious paperback copy of *The Tempest* that had fallen out of his pocket.

Allegedly, staff members and actors had, over the years, seen the ghost of this man wandering through the theatre, and was often seen pacing back and forth across the stage.

Legend, of course, had it that the ghost was there looking for the precious copy of the book that he had lost when he had fallen to his death.

Years later, I readapted the same tale for a ghost story I told to the staff at the Chapters in Ancaster during the Halloween season of 1997 – explaining how I'd encountered the ghost walking around with a copy of "The Tempest" in his hand one night.

Of course, in the Ancaster story, it was the same construction worker, but instead of falling to his death in an old theatre, he fell to his death in the construction of the Chapters bookstore.

And that his ghost could often be found pacing back and forth in a particular aisle, which happened to also be the aisle that housed the *Drama* section and included Shakespeare's plays. The ghost was, of course, looking on the shelves to see if *his* paperback copy was among the books on those shelves.

Flash forward another 10 years and the legend of Prospero's Ghost ended up finding a new life yet again.

When I was working at *Titles* bookstore at McMaster University (now known as *The Campus Store*, particularly since it doesn't have that many books in it any longer), I had purchased an Espresso Book Machine. This machine was capable of printing a trade paperback book from a digital file right on the spot in about 10 minutes. The machine printed the paper interior and the cover through two different printers, fed the two through a binding process, trimmed off the excess paper/stock and a still-warm paperback copy almost indistinguishable from a traditionally printed trade paperback book would slide out the "slot" at the end.

It was almost like a "vending machine" for books. Except you could print from one of 3 million different titles in the database.

In an attempt to promote the machine (as well as the machines at the bookstores at Waterloo and University of Alberta), we devised an anthology called *Campus Chills*. I edited the book and included horror stories from Canadian authors, all set on campuses. The first print run of the books came off our Espresso Book Machines and we help spooky Halloween-time events at the three locations in order to celebrate this collaboration and unique technology.

Wanting to have a story set at McMaster in the anthology, I thought it might be interesting to re-adapt the "Prospero Ghost" story into an academic setting at Mac. But it wasn't until I sat down and started trying to flesh out the background of the ghost with my friend and colleague Kimberly Foottit that the tale took on an entirely new light.

Prospero's Ghost was reborn and more fully fleshed out than ever before thanks to Kim's creative insights. And while we were working on making the ghost more authentic and giving him a good reason for haunting, we figured we would have some fun and incorporate the *Espresso Book Machine* at Titles Bookstore as well as the *Kirtas* scanner at the Mills Library into the storyline. We wanted to give Professor Prospero a really good reason to come back from the dead and seek his revenge on the librarians and booksellers who would dare exploit his precious text.

Working with a talented writer like Kim was just what this tale needed. I could not have pulled off the story so successfully on my own – in retrospect when I look back at it, I see how the story and characters are given greater strength and more rounded dimension with having gone through Kim's imagination and pen.

So, after almost two decades of telling the tale of Prospero's Ghost, I ended up happily landing, with my talented friend, on what I think is the penultimate version of this tale.

Though to be quite honest, I have never stopped relaying an adaptation of the original oral version of "Prospero's Ghost" set in different locales. Particularly since I regularly do talks about true ghost stories in relation to the many non-fiction books I have written.

When the mood is right, I will often share that the reason I left the bookstore at McMaster University in 2011 is because of what I saw one night while working alone on the Espresso Book Machine; how I encountered the ghost of Dr. Marshall Emerson and barely survived the eerie encounter.

Conclusion: One Last Whispering Cry

THANKS FOR JOINING me, not just in reading the stories, but in reading these stories behind the stories. I hope that you enjoyed the experience of both.

I began writing with short stories, and they will always hold a special place in my heart. In particular, short stories in the horror genre, since you can be experimental in your approach for both theme as well as format and style.

And what better way to experiment than to attempt to pay homage to some of the classics, to some of the masters who have come before me?

If you enjoyed this collection, I would greatly appreciate if you took the time to leave a review for it. It might seem like a little thing, but the one or two minutes it takes goes a long way towards helping a writer find new readers. And if you're so inclined to send me a note to let me know what you thought, that would be wonderful. My email is **mark@markleslie.ca**. (You can also sign up for my newsletter at **www.markleslie.ca** to stay informed of my new releases and get a full-sized eBook for free)

On the other hand, if you weren't satisfied with what you read, I'm happy to get an email from you just the same. Your experience and thoughts are just as important. I'm constantly looking to grow as a writer and learning why a story didn't work for a reader can be an important part of that process.

In either case, thanks for accompanying me; thanks for listening to some of those nocturnal screams along with me. Perhaps, one day, we shall encounter each other either between the digital pages of another book, or maybe in person at some bookish event. If that happens, do say hello. We might have the chance to share with one another some of our favorite classic tales.

- Mark Leslie
March 2020

About the Author

Mark Leslie is a writer, editor, and bookseller who was born and grew up in Sudbury, Ontario, spent many years in Ottawa, Ontario and currently lives in Southern Ontario. Claiming that he has always been frightened of the monster under his bed, Mark loves crafting eerie and creepy tales that follow the "what if" questions that occur to him every time he takes a peek into the shadows. And he spends a lot of times looking at the shadows and listening for the screams. You can learn more about Mark and sign up for his author newsletter at **www.markleslie.ca**.

Selected Other Books by Mark Leslie

Novels

A Canadian Werewolf in New York
Evasion
I, Death

Short Story Collections

One Hand Screaming
Active Reader
Nobody's Hero

Anthologies (as Editor)

Campus Chills
Tesseracts Sixteen: Parnassus Unbound
Fiction River: Editor's Choice
Fiction River: Feel the Fear
Fiction River: Feel the Love
Fiction River: Superstitious

Non-Fiction / Paranormal / Ghost Stories

Haunted Hamilton
Spooky Sudbury
Tomes of Terror
Creepy Capital
Haunted Hospitals
Macabre Montreal

The NOCTURNAL SCREAMS Series

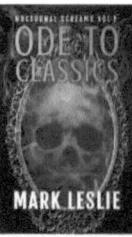